POKÉMON

POKÉMON ACADEMY

SCHOLASTIC INC.

NEW YORK   TORONTO   LONDON   AUCKLAND

SYDNEY   MEXICO CITY   NEW DELHI   HONG KONG

ISBN: 978-0-545-17722-1

Published by Scholastic Inc.
SCHOLASTIC and associated logos are trademarks and/or registered trademarks of Scholastic Inc.

12 11 10 9 8 7 6 5 4 3 2 1   10 11 12 13 14 15/0

Designed by Henry Ng.
Printed in the U.S.A.
This edition first printing, January 2010

Chapter 1

"We're going to be late, guys!"

Ash Ketchum sprinted down the country road. His friends Dawn and Brock were right behind him. It looked like any other summer morning in the Sinnoh Region, but it wasn't. It was a special day for the three traveling companions. They were on the go—and in a big hurry.

"If you hadn't overslept, we wouldn't have this problem!" Dawn yelled at Ash.

"If *you* hadn't been trying to fix your bedhead, we wouldn't have this problem!"

"Hurry!" Brock shouted at both of them.

Now they were close enough to see their destination. Up ahead was a large, low building with a walled courtyard in front. There was no one in sight as Ash and his friends raced through the entrance. They skidded to an abrupt halt.

"Looks like we made it after all!" Ash said, relieved.

"*But you're late!*"

"Huh?" Ash looked around to see who had spoken. It was Professor Rowan, Sinnoh's most famous Pokémon expert. He knew all three of them well, and he gave them a stern look. But then his mustache twitched, just a little, as if hiding a smile.

"I welcome you to the Rowan Research Facility and the Pokémon Summer Academy," Professor Rowan said. "Or, for all intents and purposes, your school!"

No ordinary school could get Ash, Dawn, and Brock to come running in the middle of summer. Professor Rowan's Pokémon Summer Academy had classes, but it was more like a camp than a school. Instead of grade levels, trainers were divided into teams. The better each trainer did, the more points they earned for their team.

Ash and his friends joined dozens of other young trainers at the other end of the courtyard.

Yuzo, Professor Rowan's assistant, called every-one to attention. "All right!" he said. He pointed to a blackboard with a list of names. "Gather 'round to find which team you're on!"

Ash, Dawn, and Brock quickly read the board. "I'm on the Red Team!" Ash said.

"Hey, me, too!" Dawn added.

Brock looked pleased. "And me!"

"Looks like *I'm* on the Blue Team," said a boy standing right behind Ash and Dawn. He was so close they could feel his breath on their necks. Surprised, they spun around.

"Conway!" Dawn despaired when she saw who it was. Yes, there was no mistaking the boy with the square glasses. Not too long ago, she had teamed up with him at a Pokémon tournament in Hearthome City. Conway was a good, smart Trainer, but he loved to sneak up on people and follow them around.

"You're here, too?" Ash asked.

Conway laughed. He was happy to see Dawn and her friends again. "Somehow, I just knew you'd all be coming!"

"Don't forget me!" Next to them, a tall girl struck a pose and giggled. "The name's Jessilinda, and I'm on the Green Team!" Her magenta hair and voice were awfully familiar. It was Jessie from Team Rocket, disguised as a young Trainer. Team Rocket had come to the Summer Academy to steal Pokémon, but Jessie had decided that being a camper was much more fun. James and Meowth were undercover, too: They were the janitors sweeping up the yard. When they saw Jessie pose, they sighed.

Everyone had found his or her team, so it was

time for a speech by Professor Rowan. Before he began, he gazed at the eager trainers in front of him. He had already met Ash, Dawn, and Brock, of course, but there were many other trainers, too. Boys and girls, bold and shy, short and tall, they had come to the Pokémon Summer Academy from towns all across the Region.

"Just as there are different kinds of Pokémon in our world, young trainers are no different!" Professor Rowan told them. "Today, you young people of differing ages and birthplaces are gathered together for a week of fun and excitement as you meet your fellow students and Pokémon. So get to know each other—and while you're at it, have some fun!"

Chapter 2

As Professor Rowan had said, the Pokémon Summer Academy was about meeting new Pokémon as well as new trainers. So even though the trainers all had their Pokémon with them, Professor Rowan's assistant brought out a box filled with Poké Balls.

"I think this would be the perfect time for the Pokémon to introduce themselves," said Professor Rowan.

"One Poké Ball per student, please!" Yuzo said, as the Trainers gathered around the box.

Ash immediately grabbed a Poké Ball, but it didn't budge. Someone else had grabbed it and wouldn't let go!

That someone else was a short-haired, sporty-looking Trainer, one of the other kids on Ash's

Red Team. "Leggo! I got it first!" the Trainer snapped.

"I got it first!" Ash shot back.

"There's nothing ruder than a guy who ignores ladies first!" the Trainer said.

"Wait!" Ash was so surprised, he let go of the Poké Ball. "You mean you're a girl?"

The girl Trainer glared at him. "Now you're really getting me mad! The name's Angie, and I challenge you!"

Well, there was nothing Ash loved more than a challenge. "Hey, you've got yourself a deal! By the way, my name's Ash!" he replied, grabbing another Poké Ball from the box.

"Good! That's the spirit!" Professor Rowan came over to the two of them. "But the order of business today is to meet the Pokémon you choose!"

"All right, then!" Angie activated her Poké Ball. "Come on out!"

"*Monferno!*" An orange Pokémon emerged from the Poké Ball. Its expression was fierce, and its tail crackled with flame. Monferno was known as the Playful Pokémon, but this Monferno didn't look playful at all.

Angie gave Monferno her biggest smile. "Angie's the name. Nice to meet you!" she said. Monferno sniffed and turned away from her.

Ash and Pikachu snickered. "Looks like you rub Pokémon the wrong way, too!"

Angie shot Ash another angry look. "Be quiet!"

"My turn!" Ash said, tossing his Poké Ball. "Come on out!"

This Pokémon was yellow, with a long, thin tail.

Ash recognized it right away: a Raichu! Raichu was the evolved form of his own Pikachu.

"Hey, a Raichu!" Ash ran up to his new Pokémon buddy. "Great! My name's Ash, I'm glad to meet you!"

"*Pikachu*," Pikachu added, trying to be friendly.

Raichu took one look at Ash and Pikachu. Then it dug a hole and jumped inside. From inside the hole, it peered up at Ash and Pikachu.

"*Rai?*" the Raichu said, too scared to come out.

Now it was Angie's turn to point and laugh. "Ash, I think Raichu's scared of you!"

"Cool it," Ash growled. "We're gonna be friends real soon!"

All the other trainers were getting along well with *their* Pokémon. Dawn and Piplup were talking to a friendly Grimer. A happy Magnemite flew in circles around Brock's head. Even Jessie as Jessilinda was cuddling a Smoochum. Except for Ash and Angie, everyone was having a great time.

Ash gave up and sat down next to Raichu's

hole. "Come out, please?" he pleaded. "What's wrong with you?"

Behind him, Angie's Monferno ran past. "Come back!" Angie called. "Where're you going?"

Her runaway Monferno stopped to growl at a Croconaw and its Trainer. The toothy blue Pokémon growled back.

"Croconaw, chill out!" its Trainer ordered, but Croconaw ignored him.

Pikachu ran between the two Pokémon to stop them from fighting. "*Pika, Pika!*" it cried.

But Monferno didn't care—it unleashed out a burst of fiery embers that charred Pikachu's fur.

"*Pika . . . Pikachu!*" Now Pikachu was angry, and it hit Monferno and Croconaw with an electric shock that stopped them in their tracks.

"Hey, don't treat Monferno like that!" Angie shouted. "That's it! I'm bringing out *my* Pokémon!"

Angie threw her own Poké Ball into the air. A graceful blue Pokémon leaped out.

"Shinx!" the Electric-type Pokémon purred.

"Use Spark on Pikachu!" Angie yelled. Shinx's fur began to glow with electrical energy. But now Ash had noticed the fight, too.

"We'll show 'em, Pikachu! Thunderbolt, let's go!" he called. Pikachu jumped into the air, surrounded by yellow lightning. "*Pikachu —*"

"*Enough!*" Professor Rowan roared, grabbing Ash and Angie by the back of their shirts. "I never told you you could use your own Pokémon in battle!"

"But Angie started the whole thing!" Ash complained.

"No, Ash and Pikachu did!" Angie protested.

"*Stop!*" the Professor roared again. He glared down at Ash. "This school is not the place for quarreling!" Then he glared at Angie. "It's for making friends with people and Pokémon!"

Angie and Ash looked at Professor Rowan in embarrassment. Even Monferno looked embarrassed. "Sorry, Professor," they sighed. The professor did have a point. And since they were on the same team, they couldn't afford to fight all the time.

Ash and Angie could argue all day, but night was a different matter. After a full day of activities, sports, and classes, it was time to get some sleep. That's what Professor Rowan and Yuzo thought, anyway.

"Lights out!" Yuzo called. "Let's hit the hay!"

"Bedtime already?" Brock said. He was in the same dorm room with Ash, Dawn, and Angie, and all four Trainers were wide awake.

"I'm not even sleepy," Ash said. True, both Ash and Angie had fallen asleep in class earlier that day. But *that* was different.

"You know," said Dawn, grinning, "I've got a deck of cards . . ."

Angie leaned down from her top bunk. "Come on, guys! Let's play!"

Conway opened the door to their room and looked in. "Say, I'd be more than flattered to be partners with Dawn . . ."

Dawn grabbed a pillow. Didn't Conway *ever* stop following people around? "Hold on, this isn't even your room!" she said, and threw the pillow at him. He yelped and ran away.

The card game began at last. As the four Trainers played, they talked.

"So, Angie," Ash said. "You haven't started on your journey yet?"

"No, I've been working in a Pokémon Day Care Center," Angie said. "It's so busy—but it's lots of fun and I'm learning a whole bunch! See, someday I'm planning to take over the business!"

"Awesome, good luck!" Ash said, and he meant it.

"What about you?" she asked him.

"Me? I'm gonna become a Pokémon Master!"

"A Master?" Angie laughed. "You? Oh, please!"

Ash rolled his eyes. "Oh man, what a mouth."

"I heard that," Angie joked. She turned to Dawn. "What about you?"

"I'm going to become a top Coordinator!" Dawn said. Piplup puffed up with pride.

"And I'm going to be a top Pokémon breeder!" Brock told Angie.

"I'll say one thing, you all dream really big—" Angie began, just as the door to their room opened. But it wasn't Conway this time, it was Yuzo!

"What part of 'lights out' don't you understand?" he shouted.

Busted! Ash and his friends threw down their cards and jumped into their bunks. "Goodnight, everybody," they whispered to one another.

Their first night at the Pokémon Summer Academy was over. But if they thought every night would be spent playing cards in their room, they were in for a big surprise!

Chapter 3

"The goal of this challenge is to give you the courage and confidence to approach Ghost-type Pokémon," Professor Rowan announced.

Ash traded looks with Brock and Dawn. Ghost-type Pokémon? That sounded spooky!

After four days at the Academy, Ash, Dawn, and Brock had met, trained, and studied new Pokémon. So far, they'd learned a lot and had a lot of fun, too. But nobody had said anything about spending the night in a creepy forest full of Ghost-type Pokémon!

Professor Rowan's assistant, Yuzo, stood at a blackboard and explained the plan. Each trainer would team up with a classmate. Together, they would cross the forest to reach the Summit Ruins. There they had to retrieve a special medal as proof of their achievement. Teams would earn points based on how quickly they reached the Ruins and found the medal.

It sounded simple enough, except for one thing: The race didn't start until seven o'clock at night. And there were lots of Ghost-type Pokémon in the forest.

"It sounds like a test of courage," Brock said thoughtfully.

Ash just grinned. "Pikachu, you ready for this?"

"*Pikachu!*" his little Pokémon responded. Pikachu was never one to shy away from a challenge.

A few minutes later, the trainers gathered in the Academy's large courtyard. Everyone was on the lookout for a good partner.

As Ash looked around, Angie's Shinx came over and greeted Pikachu. Pikachu waved hello with its paw. It was pleased to see Shinx. Even though their Trainers couldn't help squabbling, Shinx and Pikachu had become friends.

Angie wasn't far behind. "You know," she said, "since Pikachu and Shinx get along so well, what do you say we be partners?"

"Yeah!" Ash agreed. Angie might be a little hard to get along with sometimes, but she was definitely one of the best trainers at the Academy.

While Ash and his friends on the Red Team had already found partners, things weren't going as well for Conway. He needed to find someone from the Blue Team to be his partner, but he didn't see anyone around. As he wandered the courtyard, he saw a hand gesture to him from the bushes.

"Huh, you mean me?" Conway approached the bushes. A girl with dark hair and bare feet was there waiting for him. "So, you're on the Blue Team, too? And you don't have a partner?"

"Let's play together!" The girl giggled and looked up at Conway. Beneath her shaggy hair, her blue eyes had an eerie gleam. "Let's *play*!"

As their eyes met, a strange look passed over Conway's face. "Okay," he murmured.

Chapter 4

It was almost time for the race to begin. Each team was lined up at a separate entrance to the forest. Yuzo was at the Red Team's start point, ready to give Ash and Angie the signal. "Let's get rolling!" he said. "Begin!"

"Let's move!" Ash yelled, but Angie didn't need encouragement. The two Trainers ran straight into the forest. Pikachu and Shinx were right behind them.

Before too long, Ash started to slow down. "There's something creepy about this place," he muttered. Dark trees loomed overhead. Even though he and Angie had flashlights, the path around them was full of shadows.

"Just let me know if you get scared," Angie replied, still confident.

"Same goes for you, 'kay?"

As he spoke, Shinx yelped in alarm. Something had grabbed its tail! Pikachu saw something behind Shinx and reacted with a blast of electricity.

"*Haunter*!" the mystery creature cried out in surprise. It let go of Shinx's tail and dove into the bushes.

"What's wrong?" said Ash, who hadn't seen what happened.

"*Pika pika!*" Pikachu pointed at the bushes, and Ash and Angie turned to look. To their surprise, *three* Ghost-type Pokémon were crouched in the bush: Haunter, Gastly, and Gengar. They all looked terrified of what Pikachu might do next.

"I'm really sorry my Pikachu suddenly attacked you like that," Ash apologized. "Pikachu, next time, why don't you count to ten first?"

Luckily, Angie realized what had happened. "Pikachu was only trying to protect Shinx for us," she explained.

"I guess so," Ash admitted. The Ghost-type Pokémon looked like they'd rather stay in that bush, away from Pikachu's electrical attacks. So much for befriending new Pokémon—but there was still a long way to go until the night was over.

"Let's move out," Angie suggested.

"Right!" Ash agreed.

"You're off! Be careful now!" Back at the Blue Team's starting line, one of Professor Rowan's assistants watched the final Blue Team members dash into the forest. "I guess that's everybody—"

"I'm so sorry!"

To the assistant's surprise, one last Trainer was running up to the starting line.

"I'm late, I must've dozed off," the girl apologized.

"All ten of the Blue Team students are on their way to the Ruins already," the assistant explained, confused.

Now the girl from the Blue Team looked just as confused. "But you can see *I'm* not!"

"So that means — there are *eleven* students…?" the assistant asked. "Okay, well off you go, then!"

Dawn and Kendall, her partner, were already deep in the forest, headed for the Ruins. "Don't forget, if anything weird comes up I turn into a powerful protection machine!" Kendall said. He sounded brave — but he was hiding behind Dawn!

"Great. Thanks," Dawn said, trying to be polite. She didn't want to be Kendall's partner, but everyone else on their Red Team had found partners first. So when Kendall had promised to protect her, what choice did she have?

"You know," Kendall continued, glancing around nervously, "it sure gets *dark* out here."

"Shh. Listen, what's that noise?" Dawn was positive she'd heard something up ahead: a snorting, snuffling kind of sound.

"Sounds like monsters eating something." Kendall shivered. "But what? It's not gonna be *me*!"

Before Dawn could react, Kendall had taken off. He was hurrying back along the path that led to the Academy. "These leg muscles are for running!"

"Kendall, hold on!" Dawn yelled. She turned her flashlight toward the source of the sound. A Haunter, Gastly, and Gengar were having a snack on the forest path. "It's just a group of Ghost-type Pokémon and they're eating Pokémon food. That's all!"

It was too late. Kendall was long gone.

Dawn sighed and turned to Piplup. "Well, I guess it's just you and me, huh?"

No sooner had she spoken than she realized something was moving in the trees beyond Piplup. Dawn shivered, then stood up straight. She could do this on her own. She knew it.

Slowly, carefully, Dawn headed toward the trees where she'd seen something moving. But it wasn't something, it was *someone*: Conway! He was all alone. He was shuffling along, slumped over like a sleepwalker.

"Alone? No partner?" Dawn frowned. "Wonder what that's all about."

Chapter 5

This way . . . over here . . .

Conway stumbled through the forest. He didn't feel quite right, but he knew he had to follow his partner, the little girl he'd met back at the camp-grounds. She waved for him to follow her. So he did. She led him deeper and deeper into the woods.

"Okay . . . over here," Conway mumbled.

Her voice echoed in his head. *Right over here!*

Conway staggered after her. The trees thinned out to reveal they were near the top of a tall cliff. The girl walked right up to the cliff's edge. She didn't hesitate, not even for a moment.

Come on . . . come on!

The girl took one step into thin air, then another. She was floating over the darkness below. As for Conway, he just stared into space, following the sound of her voice. He didn't seem to notice the danger.

Conway took one step toward the edge, then another, trying to match the girl's pace. Then his sandaled foot stepped over the edge and he fell forward—

"*Dusknoir!*"

—and a powerful hand shot out of nowhere to grab his wrist. Conway hung there, suspended over the edge. Then he came to his senses and saw the chasm below him.

"Aah!" With the stranger's help, Conway jumped back onto solid ground, landing on his hands and knees. "You scared me!"

He looked up at his rescuer and saw a giant Pokémon floating over him. It was huge and gray, with a single ominous red eye. Its voice was deep and unearthly. "*Noir?*"

Conway yelped. Then he fainted.

The Pokémon, a Dusknoir, turned and saw the little girl — make that a *ghostly* girl — hovering over the chasm. "*Dusknoir*," it warned her, but the girl simply faded away.

A moment later, Dawn emerged from the forest to find her friend lying near the edge of a cliff. A big gray Ghost-type Pokémon stood over him menacingly, its hand on his shoulder.

"Conway!" Dawn shouted. She glared at the strange Pokémon. "All right, what did you do to Conway?" She and Piplup were ready for a fight.

"*Noir — Noir!*" the Pokémon pleaded. Then it vanished.

"Conway!" Dawn cried. "Wake up, *please!*"

Chapter 6

Conway slowly opened his eyes. "Dawn? Wha—what was that?" he mumbled. "Do you know?"

"Wait, let's see." Dawn whipped out her Pokédex. No matter what sort of Pokémon she might encounter, the Pokédex could identify it.

"*Dusknoir, the Gripper Pokémon,*" the Pokédex said. Dawn was listening attentively. "*It receives electrical waves from the Spirit World with its antenna . . .*"

That seemed normal. So far, so good.

"*. . . and is said to take people to the Spirit World as well.*"

Dawn and Conway gasped in shock.

"A few more steps and I would've ended up in the Spirit World!" Conway gasped. All he remembered was walking along with his partner and being seized by Dusknoir.

Wait—his partner! "Where'd she go? The girl I partnered with . . ."

"Huh?" said Dawn. "But, Conway, I saw you walking, and you were all alone!"

"That can't be! I was just following her!" Conway protested.

Dawn looked a little scared. "You don't think Dusknoir took her to the *Spirit World*, do you?"

"If it did, then we have a *big* problem!" The race could wait. This was an emergency!

"We're almost to the Summit Ruins!" Ash said. He'd heard some odd noises in the forest, but other than that, it had been a quiet night since the encounter with Haunter.

Mis . . .

"Angie, did you hear that?" Ash was puzzled. Another noise? Yes, they could both hear it now, a soft voice drifting through the chilly night air.

Mis . . .

Ash shone his flashlight on a large boulder ahead of them. "Sounds like it's coming from inside that rock!"

"But how?" Angie asked.

The two Trainers crept toward the rock, keeping their flashlight beams focused on it. It looked just like a normal boulder.

"*Misdreavus!*" A purple, red-eyed Pokémon sprang out from the rock. Ash and Angie shouted and fell backward, startled.

The Pokémon smiled at them gleefully.

"It's a Misdreavus," Ash exclaimed. He barely had time to recognize the Ghost-type Pokémon before it opened its mouth and shrieked.

"*Mis-drea-vus!*" The sound of Misdreavus's voice was shrill and loud, worse than nails on a chalkboard.

Ash and Angie jumped up and ran away, their hands clamped over their ears. They didn't slow down until they were too far away to hear Misdreavus's awful screeching.

"Man, you sure wimped out," Angie huffed. Both of them were bent over and out of breath.

"'Scuse me, but you ran away first!" Ash panted.

"No way!" Angie protested.

"Forget all this," Ash interrupted. This was no time for one of their usual quarrels. "We've gotta find the Ruins!"

The two Trainers straightened up. They took a good look around; after all that running, they had no idea where they were.

"Did we just get ourselves good and lost?" Angie said.

Nearby, a girl's voice giggled. Ash and Angie

turned to see a little girl waving to them from the bushes. "Over here . . . this way!" the girl called. She began to walk down the path ahead of them.

"Whoa, it's that way?" Ash brightened up. "C'mon, Angie, let's follow her there!"

Chapter 7

"Hmm, that's rather strange," Professor Rowan mused.

Dawn and Conway had returned to the Academy and told the professor all about their encounter with Dusknoir. In fact, all the trainers but Ash and Angie had returned to the Academy, and every single one reported being scared away from the forest by an angry Dusknoir.

"We monitor every Pokémon in this area, but we don't seem to have any record of a Dusknoir dwelling here," Professor Rowan continued.

"What do you think that Dusknoir's doing here?" Dawn asked.

"An accident did take place the other day," Professor Rowan remembered. He thought about the Summit Ruins. "When we were doing some renovations, we discovered a cave deep within the stone wall. There are some who think it might be the entrance to the Spirit World!"

"The entrance to the Spirit World?" Dawn repeated in surprise.

"And if in fact that's where the Dusknoir comes from, it's possible that it's attempting to take someone back with it," Professor Rowan mused.

Conway was alarmed. "I have reason to believe it may have already abducted a girl!"

The girl knew the way, all right. It wasn't long before she'd brought Ash and Angie to the Summit Ruins. Crumbling stone steps led to the top of an overgrown hill. At the top of the hill was a simple shrine built from rectangular stone slabs. Right in the open was a case — that had to be the medal!

"We finally made it!" Ash cheered. He opened the case and saw the Summit Medal inside. "Whoa, the medal!"

"Great!" Angie said. "We're the first ones!"

Ash grabbed the medal and struck a pose. "I got the Summit Ruins medal!" he said. He was as pleased as if he'd just won a Gym Badge.

Angie looked impressed. "Wow! Hey, that's a cool pose!"

"Wanna try it together?"

They each held one side of the medal and proudly held it out for the world to see. "We got the Summit Ruins medal!"

"This," Angie announced, "is *so* awesome!"

They'd completely forgotten about their guide—until they heard her giggle again. She was standing in front of a big cavern in the side of the hill. "This way, over here!"

"Is something in there?" Ash asked.

"Yes! Let's go together!" the girl called. Whatever it was, she sounded happy about it.

Ash and Angie started to follow her. But before they'd taken more than a few steps, something suddenly dropped down in front of them, its giant arms outstretched.

"It's Dusknoir!" Angie said.

Pikachu and Shinx leaped forward to defend their Trainers. A blue light surrounded them. The two Pokémon were instantly pinned to the ground.

"Was that a Psychic attack?" Angie said, worried. Then she realized what Dusknoir was really after: the little girl! "Oh no! She's gonna get hurt!"

"Stop it!" Ash shouted. He and Angie tried to run forward, but Dusknoir hit them with another blast of Psychic energy that slammed Ash and Angie to the ground.

Pikachu and Shinx growled in anger. The two Electric-types quickly shook themselves free of Dusknoir's Psychic attack.

"Pikachu, quick! Volt Tackle!"

"Shinx, use Thunder Fang! Go!"

Crackling with electrical power, the two loyal Pokémon lunged at Dusknoir. Stunned, it sank to the ground.

Dusknoir was down for the count, but for how long?

"Let's play now," the girl giggled. She hadn't budged from her spot near the cavern entrance. "Let's *play* now!"

Ash looked concerned. "Hey, this is no time to play! That Dusknoir's gonna wake up any minute!"

"C'mon, let's play together!" As she spoke, colors began to swirl at the mouth of the cavern.

A strange portal opened. "I want you all . . . *to come with me!*"

Out of nowhere, a fierce wind kicked up, blasting everything on the hilltop toward the portal. Pikachu and Shinx dug their paws into Ash's leg so they wouldn't be blown away. Before Angie could find something to hold onto, a huge gust knocked her off her feet and into the air.

Ash desperately grabbed his friend's wrist as the howling wind tried to suck her away.

"Angie! Just don't let go of my hand!" Ash yelled.

"I won't!" Angie called back. But the wind was becoming stronger and stronger. And through it all, the little girl stood at the edge of the beckoning portal, smiling.

"Come on, let's play!" she sang. "Come on! *Let's play!*"

Ash grimaced as his fingers started to slip.

Angie shook her head. "Ash, it's no use!" she cried. "Just let me go! If you don't, you'll end up going with me!"

"No way!" Ash shouted back defiantly. "I'll never give up! Even if that means forever!"

"Forever?" Angie repeated, startled.

"Let's play! Hurry up!" the girl called.

Despite his brave words, Ash felt his fingers slip again. They had to do something soon!

"*Noir noir*!" Dusknoir picked itself up and threw itself between the two Trainers and the portal. It put its arms around them as the wind tried to suck them backward. Then it turned its eye on the ghost girl.

"*Dusknoir*!" it roared, unleashing a blast of brilliant energy. The blast knocked the girl backward into the portal, where she vanished in a blaze of white light.

As the portal faded, the mouth of the cavern collapsed in a shower of rocks and boulders. In moments, the entrance was sealed.

Dusknoir gently put Ash and Angie down. The two Trainers were still gazing at the cavern in awe.

"Just a little longer and we would've ended up trapped in that cave," Ash said, stunned.

Angie turned to Dusknoir. "Dusknoir, you were looking out for us all along, weren't you?"

"*Dusknoir*," said Dusknoir, nodding.

"That's great!"

"Yeah," Ash agreed. "You're awesome after all!"

"*Dusknoir!*" the Pokémon said. Then it launched itself into the air and disappeared into the forest.

A moment later, Professor Rowan, Dawn, Conway, Brock, and several of the professor's assistants came running out of the forest.

"We finally found you! Are you okay?" Dawn asked Ash and Angie.

"Yeah, we're fine," said Angie.

"And it's all thanks to Dusknoir," said Ash.

Ash and Angie quickly told the others what had happened. When they got to the part about the portal, Professor Rowan turned and gazed at the jumble of rocks blocking the cavern entrance.

"So, Professor Rowan, you think that's the entrance to the Spirit World?" Angie wondered.

"We honestly don't know," replied Professor Rowan.

"Does that mean the girl I partnered with . . . wasn't in the Academy?" Conway asked.

One of Professor Rowan's assistants gave Conway a look. "To tell the truth, I seriously doubt that girl was part of this world!"

Conway gulped. Dawn turned to him. "I guess that means you were partnered with a ghost!"

"I was partnered with a ghost?" Conway stammered. He liked being the one who followed people and caught them by surprise. *He* did not like being the one who was followed and surprised, especially by something not of this world! "I was partnered with a — *ghost?*"

Chapter 8

The next morning, all anyone could talk about was what had happened the night before. Until Professor Rowan announced the points for last night's Ghost-type Pokémon event, that is. After a good night's sleep, even Conway had recovered from his big scare. Like the other trainers, he was looking forward to hearing the professor's announcement.

Dusknoir and the ghost girl had interrupted the event, but all the teams had gotten through the night without anyone getting hurt. Professor Rowan was so impressed he'd decided to give each team thirty points. That left Conway's Blue Team in the lead with a score of 260. Next was Jessie's Green Team with 220 points. Last was Ash's Red Team with 180 points.

Naturally, Ash and Angie were determined to make a comeback. Fortunately, there was one last event left before the Pokémon Summer Academy was over: the Pokémon Triathlon!

Ash and Angie listened intently as Yuzo explained the triathlon rules. Everyone would start at the same time, and each trainer would get a Poké Ball with a mystery Pokémon inside. Each trainer would use that Pokémon to race to the lake, where he or she would get another Poké Ball with a second Pokémon to help them across. Once the trainer had made it to the other side, it was an all-out sprint on foot to get back to the Academy and the finish line. No Pokémon battling was allowed. First place was worth fifty points, and second place would get thirty points.

"Good news for the Red Team," Yuzo added. "Your overall point total will be calculated using the points earned by all the Red Team players!"

Angie knew exactly what this meant. "That means if we do well, we'll be able to overtake the Blue Team!"

"*Shinx!*" her Pokémon cheered.

"Great!" Ash said. "We're gonna show them!"

Outside in the yard, the trainers were getting ready for the Triathlon. In Ash and Angie's case, that meant having another argument.

"Those fifty points are gonna be all mine!" Ash crowed.

"*Pika!*" Pikachu agreed.

"For your information, Ash, the Pokémon Summer Academy Triathlon is a lot more intense than you think!" Angie said.

"Go ahead and say whatever you want," Ash scoffed. "I'm gonna get first place!"

"No, that'll be me!" Angie shot back. "You'd be better off aiming for second!"

"You've got it backward!"

"I don't think so—"

"Stop! Both of you!" Dawn interrupted. Their constant bickering was really starting to get on her nerves.

"No matter which one of you finishes first," Brock pointed out, "it's the same points for our team if the other comes in second!"

"You're right," Ash admitted. He turned to Angie and stuck out his hand. "So may the best guy win!"

His sudden change of heart took Angie by surprise. Just last night he'd been ready to get sucked into the Spirit World rather than let her go, and now this? "Uh, well, uh . . ." she mumbled. She started to blush.

Ash blinked. "What's wrong with you?"

"Nothing, I'm fine!" Angie snapped, embarrassed. "C'mon, let's go!" She stormed off, followed by her confused Shinx.

"What got into her?" Ash asked.

Pikachu shrugged. It couldn't figure her out either.

Dawn watched Angie walk away. "Something doesn't seem right," she said.

Conway chose that moment to show up. "Well, Dawn, it's almost that time," he said. "I've come to the conclusion that you're going to be my most formidable rival in the Pokémon Triathlon!"

"Your rival?" Dawn was puzzled. She wasn't competitive like Ash and Angie. She'd never thought of Conway as a rival.

"That's right! I've got you marked. Exciting, eh?" Conway laughed.

Dawn was still confused. "What's up with that guy?"

Once again, Ash and Pikachu had no idea. First Angie, now Conway—but it didn't matter. They had a race to win!

Chapter 9

It was time for the Triathlon to begin. All the trainers were in position at the starting line.

"All right!" Professor Rowan called. "Everyone on your marks . . ."

"Hang on tight, buddy!" Ash whispered to Pikachu, who was perched on his shoulder.

"Get set!" *Bang*! The professor fired the starter pistol. In a flurry of feet, the trainers raced toward the first checkpoint, where an assistant waited with a tray of Poké Balls.

Jessie was first to the checkpoint, but she fumbled for a better pick. Ash and Angie simply grabbed their Poké Balls without a second thought.

"Check out my Spoink!" Ash said, as the

springy Psychic-type Pokémon emerged from his Poké Ball.

Dawn had a Dodrio, and she lost no time riding it away.

"Giddy up!" Ash climbed on Spoink's back and bounced after her.

"All right, now run like the wind, Ariados!" Angie called to her Pokémon, which scuttled along as fast as it could on its spindly legs.

Angie was behind Ash and Dawn, but she had an idea. She had Ariados use String Shot to snag an overhanging tree branch, and they swung past the others and into the lead.

"*Aria!*" her Pokémon cried.

"Eat my dust!" Angie called, gliding past Ash.

Ash growled in frustration. "C'mon, Spoink, we can't lose!"

But Angie had already reached the lake and the second checkpoint. "Thanks, Ariados!" she said, as she took her next Poké Ball and released the Pokémon inside. "All right, you're up next!"

A Lapras emerged from the Poké Ball. The big blue Pokémon floated on the lake; as a Water-and-Ice-type Pokémon with flippers to swim in the sea, it was perfect for a water race.

Angie jumped on Lapras's shelled back and the Pokémon pushed off toward the other shore. "Okay, Lapras, it's up to you!"

Ash and Spoink weren't far behind—they'd just made it to the lake checkpoint. "Thanks a lot!" Ash said, switching Spoink for his next Poké Ball. "Now it's time to clinch this!"

Back on the water, Angie could already see victory. "Grabbing first place will be a piece of cake!" she cried as Lapras sped through the water. She could feel the wind in her hair . . . and a voice in her ear. It sounded like someone was calling her name.

"Angie!" It was Ash, on the back of a Mantyke! The sleek Pokémon was just as fast as Lapras as it sliced through the water.

"Full speed ahead, Mantyke!" Ash cried.

"*Mantyke!*" the Pokémon happily responded, swimming even faster. Ash had drawn even with Angie and Lapras. In fact, it looked as if he may have pulled into the lead!

"Comin' through!" Ash told Angie, just to rub it in.

"Like that's gonna happen! Lapras, use Ice Beam, now!"

Angie's Pokémon breathed out a freezing blast that turned the water ahead of them into a giant hill of ice. Lapras slid right up the hill and sped down the other side even more swiftly than before.

The extra speed put Angie and Lapras back in the lead. "See ya later!" Angie teased.

"Huh? Quick, Mantyke, step on it!"

Now both Trainers were shouting encouragement at their Pokémon as they battled for the lead. As soon as they hit the shore, they leaped off their Pokémon and dashed for the underground tunnel that led back to the Pokémon Summer Academy.

Ash and Angie were so confident they had the lead, they were completely unaware of what was going on behind them. The competition had just taken an interesting turn, and it was all because of some unexpected competition.

Chapter 10

Jessie was not having a good Triathlon. Her first Pokémon was a Hippowdon who "raced" by burrowing underground, and that was much too sandy to be pleasant. At the lake, her second Pokémon turned out to be a Magikarp. Disgusted, she tried to throw it away, but Magikarp took off across the lake as she hung on for dear life. It was like being a water skier without the skis.

Magikarp surged right past Dawn, Conway, and Brock, then tossed Jessie onto the far shore.

As she dusted herself off, Conway popped up behind her. "I must say, that was an impressive feat," he said. He always thought Dawn was his biggest challenge, but Jessie had just outraced both of them. "It might have been a smarter choice for me to keep tabs on *you*."

Was he annoying or complimentary? Jessie decided to go with annoying. She and her Seviper ran off at top speed. She was determined to escape Conway and his Slowking. "Go pick on someone from your own planet!" she shrieked.

Conway chuckled. "Once I start keeping tabs on someone, I don't stop!"

Jessie yelped and ran even faster. But she thought to herself: *Enough with being pursued!*

"I am not losing to the likes of you, Ash Ketchum, and that's final!" Angie and Shinx were dashing through the tunnel with Ash and Pikachu by their side.

"You're gonna be changing your mind real soon!" Ash threw back at her.

At that moment, there was a shriek from behind them. It was Jessie. She and Conway ran right past them, shouting at each other the whole time.

"Seviper!" Jessie cried without missing a step. "Take care of this joker with Poison Tail!"

Seviper hissed and lashed out with its tail. Conway and Slowking jumped out of the way, but Ash and Angie were knocked over.

"That's against the rules! Stop!" Ash shouted.

Jessie ignored him. "Seviper, boink them with Bite!"

Seviper sprang at Ash and Angie, who scrambled to get out of the way. As Shinx tried to dodge, it rolled right to the edge of a nearby pit and fell in.

"Shinx, no!" Angie jumped into the pit. She grabbed Shinx with one arm and used the other to wedge herself against the pit walls so she didn't fall. "Shinx, are you okay?"

Above them in the tunnel, Jessie had hardly even noticed the danger. She just wanted Conway gone! "Seviper, make sure you pin these pinheads!" she said.

Seviper pounced at Conway, but he and Slowking ducked aside. Seviper slammed headfirst into the cavern wall, stunned.

"Sorry!" said Conway, who wasn't at all sorry. "I guess that settles that! I've won it, along with my Blue Team! My tab-keeping time with you is over!" With that, he ran off.

Jessie grabbed Seviper by the tail and dashed after him.

Back in the pit, Angie cautiously started to inch her way to the top. "I'll get us out of here, Shinx!"

"*Shinx*!" her frightened Pokémon replied.

Ash leaned over the edge and reached down to grab Angie's hand. "Hold on tight! You'll both be just fine!"

Saved by Ash again? "Thanks, Ash," Angie said,

with a little surprise and a lot of gratitude. She climbed out of the pit. Then she and Ash collapsed on the ground, exhausted.

"Thank you, Ash," Angie repeated.

"No prob!" Ash said, cheery as ever. "Glad you're fine!"

Angie's breath caught a little. That was Ash for you. A real pain in the neck, always trying to be number one, but when the chips where down . . .

"This isn't over yet!" he told her. "Let's turn this thing around!"

Pikachu was just as enthusiastic. "*Pika!*"

They got to their feet and broke into a run.

As they dashed out of the cavern, Angie said, "I'm not going easy on you just 'cause you saved me!"

"I didn't think you would!" Ash cried.

Chapter 11

"We're now at the finish line!" Yuzo crowed. He stood at the end of the race course, acting as the race announcer. "And in the lead, we have Conway! Followed by Jessilinda!"

Conway staggered into the Academy's court-yard. He was absolutely worn out! "Big mistake," he panted. "Not doing a little cardio training was pretty dumb . . ."

"*Slowking,*" his Pokémon agreed. Both of them had given it everything they had. They were so close, they could see the finish line just ahead of them. But Conway's legs were so *tired* . . .

"Put some more spring in your step, Seviper," Jessie wheezed, right next to Con-way. "Come on, like me!" She struggled to drag one foot in front of the other. Seviper didn't even have feet to step with—it just gave a weary hiss.

Behind them, they heard the sound of footsteps. And they were growing closer.

"Look at that!" Yuzo whooped. "Here come Ash and Angie!"

"That finish line was meant for *me*!" Jessie groaned.

"Almost there!" Conway tried to jog, but his legs gave out and he fell down. Jessie tripped over him. Both Trainers landed in a big, aching heap.

Ash and Angie ran right past them, shouting at

the top of their lungs. Once again, Ash was in a race to get to the Summer Academy. This time, victory was at stake! The finish line was closer, closer, and then—they were through!

"We have a winner! We have Ash and Pikachu in first place! Coming in second are Angie and Shinx! Which means the Red Team has taken first and second!"

"Yeah!" Ash said to Pikachu. "We did it!"

"Well," Angie exhaled. "So that's that. Congratulations, Ash."

Shinx purred in agreement.

"Hey, thank you, Angie! You, too, Shinx!"

The rest of the trainers crossed the finish line right behind them. Now it was certain: The Red Team had overtaken the Blue Team for first place in points!

Chapter 12

The awards ceremony was short and sweet. The Red Team had made the comeback win, but everyone at the Summer Academy received a plaque in honor of their time there.

Beneath a starry night sky, the trainers celebrated the last night of the Academy with a crackling bonfire in the courtyard. Most of the campers mingled together, eating and talking to friends both old and new.

Only Angie sat by herself. She was at one end of the courtyard, gazing at the stars.

Ash noticed her. "Angie, what's wrong?"

"It's all done," she said. When Ash didn't seem to get it, she added, "You know, over! It's the last night!"

"Yeah!" Ash realized what she meant. "Of course!"

"I must've gone to the Pokémon Summer Academy a million times before, but this year's was the best one yet," she said wistfully.

"I had a lot of fun, too," Ash said.

"You know, the most amazing thing that happened to me was that you saved me two times!"

"Well, *duh*," Ash scoffed. "I mean, you and I, we're friends!"

Angie gazed out into space. "We *are* friends, right?"

Ash stuck out a hand. "We'll meet again, no doubt."

The next morning, everyone would leave the Academy to go their separate ways. Angie would go back to work at her parents' Pokémon Day Care Center in Solaceon Town. Ash and his friends would continue their journey to Celestic Town. After all the good times — and the bickering, too — everything would be normal again.

Angie shook Ash's hand. "Yeah."

"I'll come see you the next time I get to Sola-ceon Town!" Ash promised. "I know we'll battle there!"

"And that'll be nice," Angie smiled. "Can't wait!"

Yes, she and Ash Ketchum would meet again. And they'd battle, but they'd also be friends.